LOSE . . . OR ELSE!

"You know," Travis Barnes said, "I just happened to notice that the Bulls and the Hornets play each other this Saturday. And there's something else I've noticed. Know what that is, Hopwood?"

Will shook his head.

"I'm sick and tired of watching the Bulls beat up on the Hornets, Hopwood!" Barnes shouted. "I want to see the Bulls go *down*."

"Maybe it'll happen," Will offered lamely. "Maybe this time the Bulls will lose to the Hornets."

"You *know* what I'm talking about, Hopwood," Barnes snapped savagely. "You just do what you gotta do, if you don't want me to slam-dunk you again like I did last week. And this time I won't go easy."

Will automatically touched the spot over his eyebrow. The scab was still there. He couldn't believe what he was hearing.

Travis Barnes was ordering him to throw Saturday's game!

SLAM DUNK!

by
Hank Herman

BANTAM BOOKS
NEW YORK · TORONTO · LONDON · SYDNEY · AUCKLAND

RL 2.6, 007-010

SLAM DUNK!

A Bantam Book / October 1996

Produced by Daniel Weiss Associates, Inc.
33 West 17th Street
New York, NY 10011.

Cover art by Jeff Mangiat.

ISBN: 0-553-48429-X
Published simultaneously in the United States and Canada

Bantam Books are published by Bantam Books, a division of Bantam
Doubleday Dell Publishing Group, Inc. Its trademark, consisting of the
words "Bantam Books" and the portrayal of a rooster, is Registered in U.S.
Patent and Trademark Office and in other countries. Marca Registrada.
Bantam Books, 1540 Broadway, New York, New York 10036.

PRINTED IN THE UNITED STATES OF AMERICA

OPM   0 9 8 7 6 5 4 3 2 1

To Greg, point guard deluxe

Twelve right—thirty-six left—eight right. No luck.

Will Hopwood tried it again, this time more deliberately. *Twelve. Thirty-six. Eight.* He gave the lock a hard yank, but it still wouldn't open.

Will kicked the bottom of the locker. He knew he should have paid more attention at that middle-school orientation for new fifth-graders a couple of weeks earlier—but that was still during summer vacation. How could anybody take anything seriously during summer vacation?

Now he had only three minutes until his next class—and he couldn't get his locker open!

As he was about to try the combination a third time, he felt a large hand grab him roughly by the back of the neck. "Maybe you ought to use your head," he heard a boy's voice say. Then the hand slam-dunked Will's face against the metal locker.

Oh, no, not Travis Barnes again, Will thought. He reached up to touch his forehead, just above his right eyebrow. There was a trace of blood on his fingertips.

Will turned around to face his attacker, and his fear was confirmed: It *was* Travis Barnes. Will, at five foot four, was the center of the Branford Bulls basketball team and easily one of the tallest and strongest fifth-graders entering Benjamin Franklin Middle School. He'd even grown two inches over the summer. Still, he had to look way up to see the scary face of the eighth-grader.

Barnes was nearly six feet tall. He wore his black hair long and had cold blue eyes. Nobody Will knew had ever seen him smile—unless he was picking on someone.

Travis Barnes had made a special mission of harassing Will ever since the first day of school, a week earlier. When Travis had told Will to get back to the front of the bus, Will had tried to act cocky and made the mistake of laughing at him. Well, he hadn't really *laughed* at him. He'd just thought the eighth-grader was *kidding*.

"Are you disrespecting me?" Barnes had hissed at Will. He'd grabbed Will by the belt on his jeans and the top of his T-shirt and *flung* him up the aisle of the bus toward the front, shouting, "That's where little punks like you belong!"

The previous year, as a fourth-grader, Will had been one of the coolest kids at Hawthorne Elementary School. He couldn't believe that now *he* was actually being bullied. He'd thought that at least the bus driver would stand up for him, but the driver had kept his eyes on the road, minding his own business. Will had found out later that Travis Barnes's toughness was legendary at Benjamin Franklin Middle School. Even some of the *teachers* were afraid of him.

The incident on the bus had been just the beginning. Since then, Barnes had stopped Will in the halls every time he saw him, either making fun of what he wore or demanding the Life Savers he kept in the pocket of his jeans.

The day before, Travis had grabbed Will's backpack, opened the zipper, and thrown his stuff all over the hallway. All the older kids had stood around laughing as Will got down on his hands and knees and gathered up his notebooks and papers. Will had felt like a total jerk. And on top of that, he'd been late for his next class and had been bawled out by Ms. Conte, his social studies teacher.

Now he was face-to-face with Travis Barnes again. And this time the eighth-grader's expression looked even more menacing than usual.

"Aw, Hopwood," Barnes said, as if he felt sorry for him. "Your forehead's bleeding. Here, use this to clean it up." He pulled a blue bandanna from the back pocket of his oversized jeans and held it out for Will. But as Will reached for it, Barnes let it drop to the floor.

"Well, don't just stand there, loser, pick it up!" Barnes bellowed. He was no longer using his mock sweet voice. He really sounded angry.

For a moment Will felt as though he was going to start crying. Just then he saw a familiar face. It was Mr. Neal, Jim Hopwood's favorite teacher when he had been at Ben Franklin. Jim, Will's older brother, was now a senior at Branford High.

Will was tempted to call out to Mr. Neal for help, but he knew that was the worst thing he could do. There was nothing tough eighth-graders hated more than crybaby tattletales.

Will picked up the bandanna, took a quick swipe at his forehead with it, then handed it back to Travis.

Barnes held out the bandanna and pretended to be surprised. "Hopwood, you got blood all over it! You owe me big for this. Come on—how much you got on you?"

Will emptied his pockets. He had three dollars, which was supposed to be his lunch money.

Barnes grabbed the money out of

his hand. "That's mine," he said roughly. "It'll make up a little for that crud you got on my bandanna."

The eighth-grader stuffed the bills in the inside pocket of the baggy army jacket he was wearing. Will thought he saw something in there—something that looked like a knife. All his friends had heard that some of the toughest eighth-graders carried weapons, but he'd never believed it.

"What's *that?*" Will gasped, the words tumbling out of his mouth. His eyes were bulging.

Barnes could see where Will was looking. He patted his pocket.

"Let's just say that I carry something for wise-guy fifth-graders who don't know their place," Barnes said with an uneven, twisted, sick smile on his face that made Will think of a hungry crocodile. It was the scariest look he had ever seen.

Will felt as though he was going to throw up. *Of all the eighth-graders I could have accidentally dissed on the bus,* he thought, *why did it have to be Travis Barnes?*

Will's parents had warned him all summer that now that he was starting middle school, a lot of things were going to be different. He'd have to learn to use his locker and find his way from class to class. He'd have to use his time more efficiently in order to get all his homework done. He'd have to study a lot harder.

Now, as he hurried to class, he added one more lesson himself—the most important one of all: *Keep an eye out for Travis Barnes. And when you see him, walk as fast as you can the other way!*

Will watched halfheartedly as Brian Simmons, one of his teammates on the Bulls, dribbled into the left corner of the blacktop basketball court at Jefferson Park. Then Brian launched his trademark fadeaway jumper. It was a sweet-looking shot—his form was perfect—but it spun around the rim and fell out.

"Too bad, Fadeaway, that one was halfway down. You just don't have quite the same touch at these after-school practices as you did during the

9

summer, do you?" Nate Bowman, one of the Branford Bulls' two teenage coaches, was giving Brian the business—as usual. Nate, a flashy seventeen-year-old who wore a gold stud earring, was co-captain of the Branford High basketball team, along with Will's brother, Jim. Nate was widely considered the best high-school basketball player in Danville County.

Nate and his father had nicknames for almost everyone on the Bulls, a basketball-crazed group of fifth-graders. Brian was called Fadeaway partly because of his short fade haircut, but mostly because he hardly ever missed his fadeaway jumper from the corner.

"You're right, Coach," Brian answered, wiping the sweat from his forehead. "Classes do waste too much of my energy. You're supposed to be The Man around here. Why don't you make yourself useful and see what you can do about getting rid of school?"

Will, Brian, and the other original Bull, David Danzig, had been playing hoops together since kindergarten and had known Nate for even longer than that. Though they were in awe of what he could do with a basketball, that didn't stop them from talking trash to him every chance they got.

On any other day, Will would have jumped right into the conversation too, but he'd felt unusually quiet all afternoon. While his seven teammates— Brian, Dave, Jo Meyerson, Derek Roberts, Mark Fisher, Chunky Schwartz, and MJ Jordan—were all clustered in a friendly knot under the hoop nearest the park entrance, Will had drifted off on his own near the mid-court line.

He also hadn't made a single shot yet. As a matter of fact, he already had H-O-R-S. Clearly his mind was elsewhere.

Now it was Dave's turn to shoot. He was one of the hottest ball handlers around, but it was his wide variety of shots—jumpers, finger rolls, baby hooks—that made him tough to beat in Horse. And no Bulls' practice session at Jefferson was complete without a game of Horse.

Dave started dribbling in slowly from the right side, then picked up speed as he reached the lane. As he crossed in front of the basket he whipped the ball behind his back and then laid it up softly against the backboard from the left side. He had just the right spin on it, and it fell neatly through the hoop.

"Reverse layup," Dave said coolly, "with a little mustard on it."

"Stealing my moves again, Droopy?" Nate complained. Dave's nickname, Droopy, came from the fact that his long blond hair hung down in front of his eyes and his baggy mesh shorts drooped down way below his knees.

"Nah, that move was pure DD— David Danzig," Dave answered. "I *had* to come up with something big, since

I'm the lucky guy who has *Derek* shooting after me!"

Derek Roberts, a razor-thin African American, was the most talented player on the Bulls. His father, Harold "Rebound" Roberts, was a former NBA star. Derek adjusted the red-white-and-blue wristbands he always wore and took the ball without saying a word. Derek hardly *ever* said anything—he just let his playing do the talking.

Without any fuss, Derek repeated Dave's difficult move. He also got the ball to drop through the hoop.

"That's just not fair!" Dave squawked. "He makes it look so *easy!* We gotta switch the order here. How am I ever supposed to get him out? I might as well have Jerry Stackhouse following me!"

Even Will took note of Derek's smooth behind-the-back reverse lay-up, and Will hadn't been paying attention to much of anything on the court. He'd spent most of the practice looking off into the distance. No matter how hard he tried, he couldn't get his mind off Travis Barnes. Three times already that afternoon he'd been sure he'd seen him, but each time it had turned out to be some other tall kid with dark hair.

"And I'll tell you what else isn't fair," Dave went on. "Being back in school!" Dave loved to yap almost as much as he loved to dribble the basketball. It didn't even matter if no one listened. "Summer vacation wasn't long enough. And being in the lowest grade in the school is really the pits. Don't you just love having to get out of the way every time an eighth-grader is walking toward you in the hallway?"

"Yeah," Mark Fisher agreed, shaking his head as he wiped his thick prescription goggles on his T-shirt. "They all call me Four Eyes, like they invented the name.

They think they're so funny. Ugh!"

"You don't want to *know* what they call me," Chunky Schwartz added. Chunky was the Bulls' pale, wide-bodied backup center, and his hefty build had always attracted a lot of wisecracks.

"And *me!* None of them believes my real name is Michael Jordan," said MJ, whose name really *was* Michael Jordan. Unfortunately, he was far from a natural in basketball—nothing like his famous namesake. But he *knew* more about the game than anyone around. "It really bites, being the low man on the totem pole," MJ concluded.

They should only know how much it bites, Will thought miserably as he kept his distance from his teammates and gazed off into the trees. *At least they don't have some six-foot maniac throwing their stuff all over the hallway or slam-dunking their head against the lockers!*

"Man, you guys are always *whin-*

ing," said Jo Meyerson. Jo was the younger sister of Otto Meyerson, the obnoxious star player of the Bulls' archrivals, the Sampton Slashers. When Jo first came to try out, the Bulls—especially Dave—hadn't been sure they wanted a girl on the team. But her super skills and her upbeat attitude had won them over.

"The way I see it," Jo continued as she took the ball from Derek, "is that it's September, so, hey, we go back to school." She slowly went into her dribble, getting ready for her reverse layup attempt. "The eighth-graders make fun of us, big deal," she continued. "The thing you guys seem to be forgetting is that we still get to play *basketball*. When we beat the Slashers for the championship two weeks ago, we thought that was it for Bulls' basketball till next summer."

Will, who was still in his own world at half-court, caught what Jo was saying and actually managed a half smile. It had felt good—*really* good—to stomp the Slashers in the championship. But the Danville County Basketball League had always been a summer league only, and since Benjamin Franklin Middle School didn't field a team  of its own, it had looked as though the Bulls wouldn't be playing organized hoops for a while.

Then came a big surprise—the county officials had voted to keep the league going throughout the school year. As a matter of fact, the fall season would begin in just over a week. When the news had broken, all the Bulls had been delirious.

Jim Hopwood looked at his watch. "Jo's right," he said matter-of-factly. "Knock off the whining, and let's wrap this game up. I want to get over to Bowman's before they close." From the time the Bulls were first formed, *every* practice ended with cold sodas at Bowman's Market, owned and operated by Nate's dad, the roly-poly Nate Bowman, Sr.

Jim tossed the ball in Will's direction. "Yo, little bro," he said. "Your turn."

The pass caught Will by surprise, smacking him in the chest. He'd gone back to peering off into the trees again.

Nate rapped Will lightly on the head. "Yoo-hoo," he teased, "anybody home?"

Will didn't even react to the kidding. It was as if he were in a trance. He couldn't get those nightmarish thoughts about Travis Barnes out of his head.

He snapped back into it enough to position himself just inside the foul line for a turnaround jumper, his most reliable shot. He was free to take any shot he wanted, since Jo had missed her reverse layup before him.

"Ouch! Make that oh-for-five, Too-Tall," Nate said. "You're on fire today!" he added sarcastically.

Will didn't pay attention to Nate's

wisecracks. Instead, he caught his breath as he noticed Travis Barnes leaning casually against a tree about fifty yards from the blacktop. Looking Will right in the eye, Barnes made a sinister gesture, slicing his hand across his throat. Then he moved off through the trees and disappeared.

Will looked down and noticed that his hands were shaking. It wasn't just the throat-cutting gesture that had him terrified. It was the way Barnes seemed to be *stalking* him. *How does he know where to find me all the time?* Will wondered desperately.

Though Will was standing near the foul line, surrounded by his team-mates, he was sure he was the only one who'd spotted Barnes. He was tempted to tell Nate and Jim about what he'd just seen and what was going on, but somehow he was too embarrassed. The Bulls would definitely make fun of him for being such a wimp.

The game of Horse finally ended

when Jo failed to duplicate Derek's graceful finger roll. The Bulls, who had come to Jefferson straight from school, gathered their backpacks. Nate and Jim picked up the basketballs and stuffed them into a large mesh bag with a drawstring top.

"Did you guys ever get picked on by bigger kids when you were young?" Will asked his brother and Nate as they tromped across the street to  Bowman's. He tried to make it sound as though the question were no big deal.

"I was never young," Nate cracked.

But Will's question seemed to make Jim a little suspicious. "Why do you ask?" he said.

"Just curious," Will mumbled. He tried to laugh it off and change the subject. But his throat was so dry he had trouble talking at all.

CHAPTER
3

Though it was already the third Sunday in September, the midday sun was beating down and the temperature hovered in the eighties. It felt to Will more like the middle of July. He was wearing a pair of black mesh shorts and his red Bulls jersey with the black number fourteen. On a day this hot he'd have the jersey off as soon as he started playing.

Will noticed a woman with a little boy about four years old on the sidewalk a short distance in front of him. The boy was walking a puppy, and the puppy kept running in circles around him, getting the leash all tangled up in the boy's legs. The sight made Will smile.

He realized he hadn't been smiling a whole lot lately, what with his . . . *problem*. But hey, it was Sunday, it was sunny and warm, and he had a basketball in his hands.

Will was heading for Jefferson. The Bulls had no real practice on Sunday, but some of the kids would come to the park if they didn't have to go to their grandmother's, or to some family picnic, or to wherever else parents sometimes made them go.

He turned through the two stone pillars that marked the entrance to Jefferson Park and was about to start down the narrow, paved walk that led to the blacktop. But someone was blocking his path.

It was Travis Barnes.

Will stopped. Travis lazily walked closer. The eighth-grader's eyes seemed to focus on Will's Bulls jersey for a while. Then his cold-eyed gaze traveled down to Will's new black high-tops. Will had just gotten them the week before school began.

"Nice shoes!" Barnes said, as if he were impressed—though Will knew the older boy was just making fun of him. "So new and clean," Barnes continued. "Man, it looks like they've hardly even touched the ground."

Then Barnes made a big show of looking at his own shoes. Will noticed that Barnes was wearing the same heavy, black, round-toed military-style boots and the same olive-colored army jacket he always wore—even in that day's heat. The boots were scuffed and weathered, with crusts of mud where the soles met the leather part.

"Now look at *my* boots," Barnes continued. "Nowhere near as clean as your nice, new shoes. Maybe you can help me out here, Hopwood."

With a sick feeling in his stomach, Will was positive that Barnes was about to steal his new sneakers. *Man,* he thought, *how am I going to explain to the team why I'm not wearing any shoes?* He'd have to walk home in just his socks.

But what Travis really wanted was much worse.

"Maybe you can bend down and lick my boots," Barnes said. He wore the same twisted, crocodile smile that Will had seen before.

Will tried to laugh. *He can't be serious!* he thought. But the nasty smile remained on the thirteen-year-old's face as he pointed down at his boots. He *was* serious! Will felt horrified. What was *wrong* with this guy?

He took a desperate look around, but there was no help in sight. Then he looked up at Barnes. The eighth-grader was a good eight inches taller than he was and probably outweighed him by forty or fifty pounds.

"What are you waiting for, Hopwood?" Barnes asked. While Will hesitated, Barnes lightly tapped his chest pocket—

the place where Will thought he'd seen the knife.

There was no way out. Will got down on all fours, gritted his teeth, and took a deep breath. Then he licked one of Barnes's boots. The disgusting taste, plus the very idea of what he was doing, made him gag.

"Okay, loser, now the other boot," Barnes ordered.

Will steeled himself again and took another lick. He lifted his eyes and saw two grown-ups approaching, pushing a baby stroller. Barnes, following Will's glance, also saw the couple.

"Great job," Barnes said hurriedly. "I knew you were good for something. Now go have fun at your little basketball game." Barnes started moving away from the park, toward the street. "But remember," he called back over his shoulder, "I'll be seeing you again. You can count on it."

When Barnes was gone, Will tried desperately to spit all the dirt out of his mouth. He kept spitting and spitting, but he couldn't get rid of the horrible taste.

Will could barely put one foot in front of the other as he headed in the direction of the blacktop. *It may be a sunny day,* he thought, *and I may have a basketball in my hands, but I don't see when I'll ever have any fun again— not as long as this madman is haunting me!*

"Yo, Will, move any slower and you'd be going backward!" It was Dave, calling from the blacktop. Will saw Brian and Jo there with him.

"C'mon, man, move your behind!" Dave shouted. "We need you for a little two-on-two." As Will continued to amble toward them, he heard Dave joke, "I know big men are supposed to be slow, but . . ."

Will found himself getting infuriated by Dave's good-natured yapping. *Man, that guy just can't ever keep his mouth shut!*

Will still hadn't said a word to the other Bulls. "I've got the silent man on my side," Jo piped up. "He's the tallest, I'm the shortest. That should be fair." Jo walked up to Will and placed a finger on the corner of his mouth.

Will slapped her hand away. "What are you *doing?*" he asked in a rage.

"Hey," Jo said, drawing back, "you just had something on your mouth. . . ."

Will spat in disgust.

Jo looked at him, wide-eyed. *"Calm down,"* she said. "It was just a little dirt."

The four of them stood there, staring at each other. Will had never felt more tense with his teammates than he did at that moment.

"Your ball out," Brian said to Jo and Will, breaking the awkward silence.

Jo inbounded the ball to Will, who was being guarded by Brian. Will backed him in . . . backed him in . . . backed him in . . . then finally scored easily on a turnaround jumper over Brian's head, no more than three feet from the hoop.

Brian looked annoyed. "Hey, Will, this is *Sunday* basketball," he said. "You've got four inches on me. No need to get physical."

Now the ball belonged to Brian and Dave. Dave went through a little razzle-dazzle dribble routine—behind the back, between the legs—before passing off to Brian in the left corner. Brian released a soft jumper, but Will leaped at him wildly and swatted the ball so hard that it landed about thirty yards away in the grass alongside the blacktop.

Whatever smile had been on Brian's face at the start of the game was now gone. "Hey, save that stuff for next Saturday against the Harrison Hornets, big man," he said sourly. "This is a friendly game of two-on-two, re-member?"

Will didn't answer. He just glared back at Brian.

On the next play Will again bulled his way to the hoop for an easy score. Jo, who had been open at the foul line, stood looking at Will with her hands out, as if she were still waiting for the ball.

"Are you *ever* planning to pass?" Jo complained. "Or are you going to keep posting up over Brian all day long?" The smile was gone from her face too. Nobody looked happy any-more.

Within fifteen minutes they'd had enough. Brian looked at Will. "What'd you do, take nasty pills this morning?"

Will didn't reply, but he shook his head bitterly and felt himself getting furious at his friends. *Do they all ex-*

pect me to be Mr. Nice Guy? he asked himself. *Let's see how* they'd *act if they were going through what I'm going through!*

"Let's head over to Bowman's," Dave suggested, moving toward the path. "I'm dying of thirst."

"Me too," Brian said.

"Me three," Jo added.

They looked at Will.

"I'm gonna hang here for a while and shoot around," he snapped.

"Whatever," Brian answered sullenly. He was obviously still upset about the way Will had treated him in their "friendly" game.

Will watched his teammates disappear down the path. Then he pounded the ball furiously on the blacktop. He did it again . . . and again . . . and again.

What was he going to *do?*

He could ask someone at school for help—Mr. Neal, or the principal. But he knew Barnes would destroy him if he discovered that Will had ratted him out.

He could go to Nate and Jim, but he hated to depend on his older brother to bail him out when he was in trouble. He could tell the other Bulls, but what could a bunch of fifth-graders possibly do against Travis Barnes and his buddies? He could try to take Barnes on himself . . . *yeah, right!*

Will continued to smash the ball against the blacktop. He couldn't get the taste of Travis's boots out of his mouth. He'd never felt more humiliated or furious in his life. The echo of the pounding—*thump-thump . . . thump-thump . . . thump-thump*—was the only sound he heard in the empty park.

CHAPTER 4

There was a lot of pushing and shoving and knocking off of baseball caps as the fifth-graders tumbled off the bus in front of Benjamin Franklin Middle School. Will had noticed it was always like this on Monday mornings. Nobody seemed to want to accept that the weekend was over.

"Man, Monday is the *worst,*" Dave moaned as they walked past the teachers who were standing at the front doorway, trying to keep some order.

Brian answered, "Yeah, but before

you know it, it'll be Tuesday, then Wednesday—"

"You know, Bri," Dave said in a sarcastic tone, cutting his friend off, "that makes me feel a *lot* better."

Will, who had been looking to his left and to his right as they got off the bus, now was looking back over his shoulder.

"Yo, Will," Dave said, "you got a girlfriend or something you haven't been telling us about? You spend half the day looking all around."

Yeah, I wish *that's what I was looking for,* Will thought.

Suddenly there was a loud crash directly behind them. Will actually jumped off the ground, whirling his head.

"Will, my boy, *relax,*" Brian said. "That girl just dropped her backpack. Man, you look like you've seen a ghost."

Will's face turned red. "I hardly got any sleep last night," he replied weakly. "I guess I'm a little jumpy."

Just as Will was recovering from the surprise of the sudden noise, he caught sight of Travis Barnes looming at the end of the hallway. He had *known* it was too good to be true when he hadn't seen Barnes on the bus that morning. The eighth-grader must have gotten a ride to school.

In a weird way, Will almost felt relieved to have finally spotted him. *Seeing* him was better than *worrying* about seeing him.

Barnes looked down at Brian and Dave as they approached. "Excuse me, you two," he said in a mocking, overly polite tone. "Do you mind if I talk to your friend Hopwood alone?"

Brian and Dave looked at Will questioningly, and he nodded back at them. "Fine with me," Brian said over his shoulder to Will as he and Dave moved on ahead.

Will wanted to get this thing over with as fast as possible. He was sure he knew what Barnes was after. "Okay, how much do you want this time?"

Will asked resignedly, reaching into the pocket of his jeans.

Barnes looked at him with that sick smile. "Take it easy, Hopwood," he said, sounding almost friendly. "What makes you think I'm after your money?"

Will didn't say anything.

"You know," Barnes continued evenly, "ever since the first day of school, when you made that, uh, little *mistake* of laughing at me on the bus, I kinda thought you looked familiar. Then yesterday at Jefferson, seeing you in that red jersey, I put it all together. You're on the *Bulls*."

Will waited. He didn't understand how his being on the Bulls was a problem for Barnes.

"My cousin is Elvis Bailey," the eighth-grader went on. "He's the center on the Harrison Hornets."

Elvis Bailey. Will slowly formed a picture of him in his mind. *That awkward, ugly kid with braces—the one I eat for lunch every time we play Harrison. . . .*

"Starting to see the connection, Hopwood?" Barnes asked. "You know, I just happened to notice that the Bulls and the Hornets play their first league game against each other this Saturday. And there's something else I've noticed. Know what that is, Hopwood?"

Will shook his head. There was something in Barnes's voice that gave him a sinking feeling. He felt as though the eighth-grader's blue eyes were looking right through him.

"It's that the Bulls always win," Barnes said flatly.

"Yeah. Uh, I guess we do," Will answered. He didn't know exactly where Barnes was leading, but he was pretty sure he didn't want to find out.

The older boy's tone of voice had changed. There was no trace of friendliness left in it. "I'm sick and tired of watching the Bulls beat up on the Hornets, Hopwood!" he almost shouted. "I want to see the Bulls go *down*."

The way Barnes said it made Will's knees feel weak. Will also noticed that a lot of the other kids in the hallway had stopped to stare. But Barnes turned around to glare at them, and the crowd scattered.

"Maybe it'll happen," Will offered lamely. He wished more than anything that Barnes would just leave him alone. "Maybe this time the Bulls will lose to the Hornets."

"No, Hopwood, you still don't understand," Barnes growled, his face so close that Will could feel the heat of his breath. "The Bulls *will* go down. No *maybe*. Get it?"

"What are you talking about?" Will asked in a pleading way.

"You *know* what I'm talking about, Hopwood," Barnes snapped savagely. "You may be a punk, but you're not a dummy. You just do what you gotta do, if you don't want me to slam-dunk you again like I did last week. And this time I won't go easy."

Will automatically touched the spot over his eyebrow. The scab was still there. He couldn't believe what he was hearing.

Travis Barnes was ordering him to throw Saturday's game!

Will stood motion-less as Barnes strode off down the hall. Then, still in a daze, he staggered forward to catch up with Dave and Brian.

"Nice of you to hook up with us lowly fifth-graders again," Dave joked. "I'm surprised you still have time for us, now that you hang with the eighth-grade studs."

Will desperately attempted to pull himself together as Dave kidded him. He tried to put a nonchalant look on his face.

"What did Big Bad Barnes want with you, anyway?" Dave pursued. He didn't seem to want to let up on the subject, though Will wished he would. "You two dudes were talking for a *long* time."

Will puffed out his chest in an exaggerated way. "He just wanted to know how I got so cool so fast."

Dave pretended to choke. "Yeah, *right,*

Hopwood," he sputtered. "I'm sure that's *exactly* what he wanted to know."

Throughout the exchange with Dave, Will felt Brian's eyes on him. *Has Brian figured out that what's going on between me and Travis is a whole lot scarier than some innocent wisecracking?* Will wondered.

He hoped not. The *last* thing he wanted was for any of the Bulls to know how terrified he was.

CHAPTER 5

"Dad, you gotta make a *right* here!"

Mr. Hopwood stepped on the brakes and was able to slow down just enough to make the turn his son Jim had indicated.

"After all this time, you still don't know where the Harrison Community Center is yet?" Jim asked impatiently.

Mr. Hopwood smiled across the front

seat at his wife. "Jim," he said over his shoulder, "ever since you started driving, you know all the answers."

"Hey, you didn't even need to take us, Dad," Jim pointed out. "I would have driven. And I bet Will would've preferred that, anyway, right, Will? Will?"

No answer.

"Earth to Will," Jim said a little louder.

"Oh yeah, right," Will answered, startled. He'd been only half listening to his family's conversation.

"How do you guys figure to do against Harrison?" Mr. Hopwood asked. He left the question open for either of his sons.

"We'll kill 'em," Jim answered simply. "We already beat 'em twice over the summer."

"Well, we'll be cheering for you from the stands," Mrs. Hopwood said.

"It should be a great game," Jim continued. "Will *owns* that kid Elvis Bailey." Jim looked over at his younger brother to see if his psych job was working. But again there was no reaction.

"Yo, Will," Jim shouted, punching him in the arm. "Wake up. We're almost there. You planning to play, or what?"

Will knew he was supposed to say something. "Yeah, let me at those guys," he replied unconvincingly.

Will overheard his father saying something to his mother in a low voice about how oddly Will had been behaving lately. He hated when they talked about him and he wasn't supposed to hear.

"What's the matter, honey?" his mother then asked him directly, in her normal voice. "You haven't been yourself. What is it? Are you having trouble getting used to the new school? Because if you are—"

"I'm not having trouble getting used to the new school!" Will exploded from the backseat.

He was furious. Furious at his parents for being so off the mark.

And furious at himself for not being able to tell anyone about what was really going on.

Since this was their first game as the champions of the league, the Bulls started off psyched. But the game wasn't turning out the way they had expected. And Will knew that it was obvious to everybody that he was to blame; he just wasn't playing his best. After the first quarter they were down 13–8. Now, with four minutes to go in the second, it was Harrison 21, Branford 15.

Jo punched the ball into Will in the paint. Elvis Bailey guarded him closely. "Come on, hotshot," Bailey taunted. "Show me what you got."

Bailey had been baiting Will from

the opening tip. He had told Will that it was "payback time," that in this game it would be "all Hornets." Will had realized immediately that Elvis was in on the threat his cousin had made and was trying to use it to his advantage. He found it very upsetting that someone else—someone on the *Hornets*—knew what had gone on in private between him and Travis Barnes.

Will began to back Bailey in. Though the Hornets' center was almost as tall as he was, normally Will would have used his strength advantage to muscle in for the short turnaround jumper. But this time, after one dribble, he kicked the ball back out to Jo on the perimeter.

"Come on, Will!" he heard Jim snap. "You had position! You should take that guy every time!"

"Hey, Hopwood," Bailey snickered as they jockeyed for rebounding position. "Big brother's not too happy with your sissy play, is he?"

Will wanted to deck the big, ugly kid. He was talking tough only because he had Travis Barnes to back him up.

Jo skidded a hard bounce pass over to Derek on the right wing. Derek faked a jumper, then sliced through the lane for a pretty  layup, cutting Harrison's lead to four.

Devon Haskins, the Hornets' skinny, left-handed point guard, walked the ball up the floor, surveying the Bulls' defense. Three passes later, the ball was in the hands of Elvis Bailey, down low on the right blocks. Without hesitating, Bailey went right at Will with a lean-in jumper. Will put his hands up but didn't offer any real resistance.

"Nice D, Hopwood," the meaty center sneered. Will could see his braces gleaming. Bailey's macho act was really eating away at him. If only he could grind the Hornets' center up the way he always did!

Dave pushed the ball upcourt for the Bulls. He put his fist in the air, indicating a set play.

Will, however, didn't see the fist. In the first quarter he had caught sight of Travis Barnes sitting on the bleachers near the Hornets' basket. Now Will couldn't stop himself from looking over at Barnes every few minutes. He also constantly heard him yelling things like "Bulls bite" and "Today's the day, Hornets. I *know* it is!"

This time when Will caught his eye, Barnes was wearing that crooked, crocodile smile of his and nudging his muscle-bound buddies. Will thought he saw him pat his chest pocket, but he wasn't sure.

"Will!" he heard Dave call. Dave was pulling the ball back out to reset the play. He sounded really annoyed. "You were supposed to set a pick. C'mon, get with the program!"

When Will failed to move, Dave hoisted up a long shot, but it was out of his range. The ball clanged off the

back iron. Will was in decent position for the rebound but was shoved out of the play by Elvis Bailey, who came down with the ball.

"Playing kinda soft today, aren't you, hotshot?" Bailey gloated as he swung his elbows.

Will wanted to yell something back, but he had nothing to say. Bailey was right: He was playing soft. No way he wanted the Bulls to lose. He *wanted* to play with his usual kind of fire. He just . . . *couldn't.*

Will ran back on defense and set up in the paint. Haskins, the Hornets' point guard, lost Dave with a spin move, then drove to his left, straight at the hoop.

Will knew he should step in front of the guard—maybe draw a charge, or at least force him to pull up and settle for a jumper. But he was frozen to his spot on the floor. The lefty coasted right by him for an easy layup.

Without actually seeing it, Will could feel Dave's accusing gaze. *You don't even have to tell me,* he felt like saying. *You think I feel good playing like a pushover?*

As the two points were being rung up on the scoreboard for the Hornets, widening the gap to 25–17, Will ran by the section of the bleachers where Travis Barnes and his buddies were cheering along with the other Hornets' fans. He heard Barnes yell,  "All *right,* Hornets! You can *take* those Bulls. *It's in the bag!*" Then to Will he added with a wink, "Ain't that right, Hopwood?"

There was less than a minute to go in the half. Jim signaled for a time-out.

On the way to the Bulls' bench, Brian asked Will sharply, "What was

48

that all about between you and Travis Barnes?"

Will waved his hand, trying to dismiss the question. "Just his normal garbage. No big deal." Will made a point of looking down at his sneakers, but Brian wouldn't stop staring at him.

"Okay," Jim said to the Bulls, who were huddled around the coaches. "We've got thirty seconds left, and we're down by eight. Let's see if we can hold for one good shot and cut that lead to six before the break." Then, looking directly at his brother, he added, "Will, you've got a lot of making up to do. It's time to step up."

He turned his attention to the Bulls' guards. "Dave, Jo, kill some time up top, then get the ball to Will. We'll clear out and let Will go one-on-one with Metal Mouth."

Jim waited for Will to respond, but he didn't say anything.

"Come on, Will," Jim prodded one more time, "that goon's been making you look bad all afternoon. What's the matter with you today? *Take* him this time!"

Will briefly thought about telling his brother the problem—it would be such a relief to tell *someone*. But he just couldn't. He had to deal with Travis Barnes by himself.

Nate gave each of the Bulls a pat as they headed back onto the floor. He held his hand on Will's back just a little bit longer. "Come on, guys. Show time!" he yelled.

Jo inbounded the ball to Dave, and the two of them exchanged a few un-challenged passes above the three-point circle. They were letting the clock run down, as Jim had in-structed.

With twelve seconds to go, Jo whipped an over-the-head, two-hand pass to Will, who was positioned to the right of the foul line. The rest of the Bulls shifted to the left side of the court, leaving Will isolated against Elvis Bailey.

Will eyed Bailey, then threw a pump fake. Bailey bought it. He left his feet in a wild attempt to block the shot and couldn't avoid coming down on Will.

"Foul, number twenty-two," the ref called. "Two shots."

Will stepped slowly to the line. He knew he had to concentrate and put all that other stuff out of his mind. He'd deal with that later—somehow.

But just before the ref handed him

the ball, he remembered Travis's words: *The Bulls will go down!*

Will looked around and saw Barnes near the Hornets' basket. Their eyes locked. Then Barnes made a quick gesture with his hand across his throat.

Will tried to steady himself. He flexed his knees, bounced the ball on the floor three times, then spun it in the air to get just the right feel. But his arms felt rubbery.

His first shot fell short, barely grazing the front rim.

Gotta focus, Will told himself. *Forget all that other stuff.*

As he pounded the ball on the floor, preparing for his second shot, his eyes drifted to Elvis Bailey, who was standing along the lane in position for a rebound. Bailey was smirking.

Will put up the shot, but it didn't

feel right leaving his fingertips. It hit the back of the rim, then spun around and around and around . . .

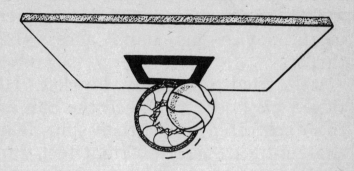

No good.

CHAPTER
6

Mark Fisher wiped his goggles on his shorts and didn't stop until he could see himself in them.

Derek Roberts ripped off his soaking red-white-and-blue wristbands and chucked them into his gym bag on the locker room floor. Then he took out two fresh ones and smoothed them onto his wrists.

Dave tugged at his blue shorts until the bottoms hung exactly midway between his knees and the tops of his sneakers—just the way he liked them.

All the Bulls went through their halftime rituals. They did whatever they could to make themselves feel comfortable, because the score—Harrison 25, Branford 17—was not very comforting.

Will sat on a bench with his head hanging down between his knees. He had never felt so totally miserable in his life.

Nate and Jim were talking in the john, near the door of the locker room, and Will could just barely make out their conversation. "Down by eight to the *Hornets?*" he heard Jim saying. "What are we gonna do with these guys?"

"I'll tell you one thing we gotta do," Nate answered. "We gotta light a fire under that kid brother of yours. He's been *invisible* out there."

Thanks, Will thought. *Just what I needed to hear.*

As Will sat trying to rally enough strength to go out for the second half, Brian threw an arm around him and led him off to a quiet corner of the locker room. Will followed as if he were sleepwalking. "Hey, buddy," Brian said as they moved, "you and me gotta talk."

When they were out of earshot of the rest of the Bulls, Brian looked Will right in the eye. "Okay, let's have it. What's up, man?"

"What do you mean?" Will replied. He wasn't sure how much Brian really knew, and he didn't want to give anything away yet. "You talking about those two free throws I blew? That was just—"

"No, I'm not talking about the free throws," Brian cut in. "You know what I'm talking about. You and Travis Barnes. You've been walking around like a zombie ever since Barnes stopped you in the hall last Monday—and come to think of it, maybe even before that. I knew something was up, but you had to be too cool to let me in on it."

So Brian had *figured out that something big was going on between me and Barnes. Man, he doesn't miss a trick!* Will thought. He felt a weight lift off his chest. Maybe he wouldn't have to go through this all alone after all.

"And *today*, man," Brian went on, "that's not *you* out there. Okay, you missed a few shots—I've certainly seen you do *that* before . . ."

Will laughed nervously.

". . . but playing like a wimp? That's not the Will Hopwood I know. I haven't seen you play that soft since we were in kindergarten!"

Will smiled broadly. Here Brian was insulting him, yet he felt so . . . *relieved!* He actually felt tears coming, but he choked them back. Since Brian already knew something was up, now he could tell him *everything!*

Will pushed Brian even farther into the corner, so they were almost in the shower stalls, and looked around over his shoulder. He still wasn't ready for the rest of the Bulls to hear this yet.

"Listen," he began in a frenzied whisper. "Elvis Bailey? He's Travis Barnes's cousin!"

"Yeah?" Brian replied. "So?"

"So Barnes is sick of seeing the Hornets lose to the Bulls. And he's sick of seeing me school his ugly cousin every time we play them!"

"And?" Brian prodded.

"And he threatened to slam my head against the locker—only a lot harder than last time."

"*Last* time?" Brian asked. "How long has this been going on?"

"A while," Will admitted. "He's been a total jerk to me lately." Will paused and took a deep breath. "And he also threatened me with his knife—"

"His *knife?*" Brian jumped in, alarmed. "How do you know he carries a knife?"

"*Everyone* knows he carries a knife," Will answered. "I've even seen it." Though this wasn't altogether true,

Will had convinced himself it was. He felt so relieved at finally being able to talk about Barnes that he was about to mention the shoe-licking incident— but stopped short. That was too disgusting even to think about.

"Okay, now slow down," Brian said, rubbing one hand over his short fade haircut. "Travis Barnes threatened to slam-dunk you and cut you . . . if *what?*"

"*If the Bulls win!*" Will almost shouted. "I'm supposed to throw the game!"

Brian stared at him, his eyes bugging out. "That's really bad!"

"I know, I know," Will said, his voice shrill. Then he saw Chunky Schwartz and some of the other Bulls looking in their direction from the benches. He lowered his voice. "I mean, I haven't been *trying* to throw the game. I just can't seem to *play!*"

"I didn't mean that what *you're* doing is really bad, knucklehead," Brian explained. "Of *course* you can't play. I meant it's really bad that Travis

Barnes would do that to you. What an animal! He's worse than I thought."

"You have no *idea*," Will said slowly, shaking his head.

"Will," Brian asked, "why haven't you told Jim and Nate about this? They'd cut that loser down to size in a second. And I'd love to be there to see it!"

"Bri, you don't understand," Will replied. "I don't want to go crying to my older brother. You know how that would look around school? Besides, I'm too old for that."

"Great—so what are you gonna do?" Brian pursued. "Take Travis Barnes on all by yourself?"

Will just stared back at Brian. Finally he shrugged and looked down. "I don't know," he mumbled.

"Well, just remember this," Brian went on. "Whatever you decide to do, however you decide you want to handle it, the Bulls will stand behind you. I can promise you that."

Brian extended his hand down

below his waist, and Will slapped him a low five, the traditional gesture of the Bulls.

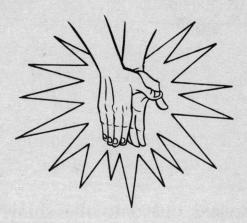

Then the two boys headed for the door of the locker room. It was time to face the Hornets.

Will walked out onto the shiny wood floor for the second half feeling as though someone had just let him out of jail. Finally being able to spill his problem to Brian had made a huge difference.

But as he crouched to defend against the Hornets' inbounds pass, he heard a sharp voice calling out, "Hey, Hopwood. Game's only half over. Still got some work to do."

It was Travis Barnes, of course, and *boom!* The voice brought him back to reality like a punch in the midsection. Though he had *shared* his problem with Brian, Will realized he hadn't done anything about *solving* it.

While Will was trying to sort out his jumbled thoughts, the Bulls got off to a quick start. Dave knocked down a three-pointer and Derek connected on a gorgeous underhand scoop, cutting the Hornets' lead to three.

But the Hornets answered right back. Devon Haskins hit a running one-hander in the lane, and Drew Schulz, the Hornets' redheaded shooting guard, canned a shot from the right corner.

Hornets 29, Bulls 22.

In those first few minutes, Will got a sense of how the second half was going to go. The Bulls had come out slugging, but the Hornets, beginning to smell an upset, were not about to roll over and die.

Midway through the third quarter, Elvis Bailey rebounded a missed free throw by Haskins, but Will got his hands on the ball at almost the same time. As they tangled for possession, spinning each other around, Bailey was thrown to the floor. Though Will had wrestled for the rebound ferociously, now he stood over his opponent with an apologetic look on his face.

He saw Bailey looking up at him. The Hornet's expression, surprised when he had hit the deck, had now turned furious. He kept staring at Will.

"Outlet!" Will heard Dave call impatiently. Will finally snapped out of it and threw a long pass to Dave, who was heading upcourt on the left side. As he released the pass he heard a no-nonsense command from the bleachers.

"Watch it, Hopwood!" It was Barnes again, Will knew, and this time there was an unmistakable threat in his voice.

The Bulls were unable to work the ball in for a good shot, and finally Mark Fisher, who was in the game for Jo, heaved one up from downtown. It actually rolled around the rim, but finally it dropped out.

Haskins quickly brought the ball upcourt for the Hornets, then lobbed a pass to Bailey in the pivot. Bailey turned around and drove right at Will, who backed off, allowing him to hit an easy eight-footer.

"That's more like it," Will heard Barnes murmur approvingly.

At almost the same time he heard Jim thunder, "Step in front of him, Will! Stop playing like a wimp!"

Through the rest of the third quarter, Will felt like a pinball bouncing from bumper to bumper. There was one voice warning him to back off. There was another shouting at him to play tough. There were his parents, sitting with the other Bulls' parents in the bleachers, cheering him on. There was his natural instinct to shut down Bailey. Then there was the image of Barnes, his cold blue eyes, his big fists, his knife . . .

At least he was able to score four points in the period. That was four more than he'd had in the whole first half.

The third quarter ended with the Hornets leading the Bulls, 36–31.

At the Bulls' bench, Jim was more hyper than usual. "Let's keep up the intensity—and even pick it up a notch. The Hornets may have started the game strong, but they're starting to fade now. I can feel it!"

MJ, who pretty much thought of himself as the Bulls' third coach, added, "Besides, we *always* beat the Hornets, and the Hornets know it. And don't think they *forgot*, either!"

Now it was Nate's turn. Nate was never down, but when things started to get exciting, he got into it more than anyone. "All right, Droopy," he chimed in, addressing Dave, "you're gonna make ol' Devon Haskins look like Devon Has-been. Derek, my man, you're gonna be taking it to the hole, Michael Jordan style. And Too-Tall," he bubbled, wrapping his long arm around Will's shoulders, "you're gonna chew up and spit out that nasty-looking Bailey dude, the way you always do!"

Will could tell Nate was expecting a response, but all he could do was stare down at his shoes.

Brian came to his res-cue, extending his hand into the middle of the huddle. "Come on, guys," Brian chanted, "let's do it!"

All the Bulls put their hands in. "Show time!" they yelled.

The noise level in the Harrison Community Center rose as soon as the teams stepped onto the court for the fourth quarter. The home team fans felt they might be eight minutes away from a surprising victory, and they were doing everything they could to help their team.

Will's head was swimming. Again the chorus of voices collided in his brain: *Chew him up and spit him out. . . . Stop playing like a wimp. . . . Watch it, Hopwood. . . . The Bulls will go down—do what you gotta do. . . .*

It was the Hornets' ball to start the fourth quarter. Devon Haskins nonchalantly pranced up the floor with his show-off high dribble. Then he got down to business and fired a pass into the right corner to the Hornets' tall, stringy forward. The forward skipped a bounce pass to Bailey down on the right blocks.

Bailey wheeled toward the basket and shot, but Will timed his leap perfectly and with a thunderous

THWACK sent the ball careening into the bleachers.

Nate instantly bounced to his feet on the sidelines. *"Rejection!"* he screamed. "That's the way to defend! That's the way to get physical, you animal! I *love* this game!"

The block had made Will feel great too—for the moment. Then Elvis glared at Will and hissed, "You're going to regret that, Hopwood." Immediately a cold, sweaty feeling came over Will again. It was as if someone had stuck a pin in him, letting all the air out.

The next time the Bulls had the ball, Nate called for a clear-out: Four Bulls would shift over to the left side of the floor, bringing their defenders with them. That would leave just Will on the right side, to go one-on-one against Elvis Bailey.

Will threw a halfhearted ball fake, but Bailey didn't fall for it. Then he tried a pump fake, but his opponent didn't buy that one, either. Finally he passed the ball weakly over to Dave on the other side of the floor.

"Too-Tall!" Will heard Nate moan in disappointment. "You can take him any day! What's *wrong* with you, man?"

Both teams continued to go at each other in the fourth quarter, but the Bulls' superiority finally began to show. Derek and Brian caught fire at the same time, and the Hornets' lead dwindled.

With sixteen seconds to go in the game, it was Hornets 46, Bulls 45. And it was the Bulls' ball. One basket was all it would take.

Dave moved the ball up the floor deliberately—no behind-the-back dribble on this trip. Haskins picked him up at half-court, but Dave managed to lose the Hornets' guard on a solid pick set by Jo at the top of the key. As

Dave exploded through the lane, two Hornet defenders flew at him. Sensing the double-team, Dave alertly dished the ball to Brian, who was wide-open in the left corner, his favorite spot.

Four seconds on the clock. Brian took time to line up his shot. Then he launched a beautiful, high-arching soft jumper that went in . . . and out!

The rebound came down in the hands of Elvis Bailey, who gleefully held the ball up over his head, waiting for the buzzer to sound. He fixed Will with a disdainful sneer.

It was too much. Something in Bailey's taunting expression made Will snap. *Just who does this ugly loser think he is?* Suddenly Will didn't care anymore about Barnes, the knife, the threats. Seeing the way Bailey waved the ball in the air, unprotected, Will leaped like a Doberman and ripped the ball from his grasp. Then, without hesitating, he went right back up with his trademark fallaway jumper.

The Bulls had beaten the Hornets again!

As the buzzer sounded, Brian, Dave, Jo, and Derek—as well as the three Bulls on the bench—all rushed Will and lifted him onto their shoulders. Jim and Nate grabbed each other and jumped up and down in the middle of the court like a pair of kindergartners.

Will too felt ecstatic—until he glanced into the bleachers.

There he spotted the beet-red, furious face of Travis Barnes glaring down at him.

CHAPTER 8

"All right, Too-Tall," Mr. Bowman said as Will and Brian were leaving the store after the Bulls' victory celebration, "no more of these buzzer-beater finishes." He tapped his chest. "No good for my heart." Mr. Bowman had suffered a heart attack during the summer, and that had thrown quite a scare into all the Bulls. "Now listen, you two," Mr. Bowman continued, "I want you both to head straight home. Your parents trusted me to look after you tonight, and it's starting to get dark earlier these days."

The balding shopkeeper thought of all the Bulls as his sons, almost the same way he thought of his own son, Nate, Jr. A former player himself, Mr. Bowman loved to hear every detail of all their games, and sodas were on the house when the Bulls won. That day's celebration had been particularly noisy, since it followed a win that the Bulls hadn't wrapped up until the final seconds.

As the two boys crossed the street to walk along Jefferson Park in the fading sunlight, Brian said to Will, "Hey, I know you didn't want to talk about this inside with the guys, but you made the right decision. You know, going for the win."

Will chuckled. "I don't know if I'd call it a *decision,*" he answered. "It just kind of *happened.* You know, when you're as good as I am . . ."

"Well, whatever," Brian said. "I just

wanted you to know that you did the right thing."

"Easy for you to say," Will replied with a thin smile. "*I'm* the one who's gonna get beat up." Though Will still spoke in a kidding tone, the light, happy mood from the victory celebration was starting to fade. The queasy feeling that had been with him all week was beginning to take its place.

There was absolutely no doubt in Will's mind that he'd be running into Travis Barnes on the way home. He mentioned this to Brian.

Brian hesitated, then said what was on his mind. "You know, Will, I *told* you I thought you should get Jim and Nate in on this, and I *still* think—"

"We've been *through* that," Will said, cutting him off impatiently. "I already told you—I've got to handle this Barnes thing myself."

"All *right*, all *right*," Brian responded, holding up his hands. "Forget the Jim and Nate idea. At least you'll have *me* to protect you."

For a split second Will was amused. The thought of him and Brian taking on Travis Barnes and his posse almost made him laugh. But his mind was made up.

"Sorry, Bri," he said. "You go home your way, and I'll go mine. We'll talk tomorrow." Then, with a grim smile, he added, "I *hope.*"

To make sure there was no further discussion, Will started walking off. Of course he wished he had Brian's company, but he knew he was doing the right thing. *What's the point of the* two *of us being knocked silly?* he figured.

Will covered the three blocks to the end of Jefferson Park without looking back. He didn't want to give Brian any encouragement to tag along.

At the edge of the park, Will turned the corner—and there they were: Travis Barnes and the same three eighth-grade buddies who had been at the Bulls-Hornets game. Will noticed that none of them was small—and none of them looked happy.

This is it, Will thought. *This is what Barnes warned me about.* The Bulls were supposed to lose, and they hadn't. Now he'd have to deal with the consequences. He drew in a long, deep breath.

Barnes slouched with his back against Jefferson Park's stone wall, menacingly punching one palm with the other fist. "Well, if it isn't *my hero*," he said sarcastically to Will. "Nice job today, Hopwood," he continued, "but I thought we had an understanding. Didn't forget about that, did you?"

"Hey, I just played my game, like I always do," Will answered. Then a strange urge overcame him, and he added, "If your cousin stinks, and so do the rest of the Hornets, that's not my problem." Will figured he was in for a beating anyway, and he might as well get his money's worth.

"Oh, but I think it *is* your problem," Barnes said darkly. He and his crew had formed a ring around Will, and now they were beginning to close in on him.

Suddenly Barnes grabbed Will by the shoulders and sent him flying across the circle to one of his buddies, who caught Will with a knee in the midsection.

Will crumpled to the sidewalk in pain, momentar-

ily unable to breathe, but Barnes pulled him back to his feet. "Hey, come on, Hopwood, you're a *hero*," he taunted. "You don't want people to see you rolling around on the ground." As he talked, one of his cronies sneaked behind Will and got down on all fours. Barnes gave Will a hard shove, and Will fell backward over the crouching kid.

"Oops, down again," Barnes mocked. "Just can't seem to stay on your feet, can you?" All the eighth-graders snickered.

As he tried to get up, Will saw a group of kids rushing around the corner and coming in his direction. It was Brian and Dave, followed by the rest of the Bulls.

Barnes noticed them at the same time. "Now isn't this *cute?*" he said mockingly to his sidekicks. "The rest of the little Bulls. One for all and all for one."

Will looked at Brian. "I told you I wanted to handle this on my own," he said under his breath.

"Wait a minute," Brian replied. "We're just here to make sure it's a fair fight." Then he looked at Barnes accusingly. "And so far all I've seen is four eighth-graders pushing around one fifth-grader."

Will, who had climbed back to his feet, waited for Barnes's reaction. Gradually the uneven, twisted smile appeared on his enemy's face.

"So it's a fair fight you want?" Travis asked Brian. "Man-to-man? Hey, no problem." He motioned for his buddies to back off.

Then, without any warning, he whirled and belted Will in the stomach. Will doubled over, but Barnes yanked him upright and smashed him hard on his right arm, just below the shoulder. The blow sent Will stumbling back against the brick wall.

Before Will could begin to defend himself, the six-footer charged him again. This time he delivered a head butt to Will's chest. Feeling as though he'd been smashed with a sledge hammer, Will collapsed to the sidewalk again.

When he looked up, he saw Barnes's cold blue eyes staring down at him, silently challenging him to stand. He tried to make it back to his feet, but his legs were too wobbly.

"Come on, Hopwood, take it like a man," Barnes taunted, pulling him upright again. "Oh, and one more thing," he added. "When you're walking on my turf, you really don't want

81

to be wearing a *Bulls'* uniform."
Barnes took hold of Will's red jersey
by the scooped neckline and gave a
hard yank, ripping the shirt all the
way down the front.

Will's eyes narrowed to slits, and his
fists clenched. Mr. Bowman had given
the Bulls their jerseys! Barnes had
gone too far. *Nobody* was going to get
away with that!

Will's fear was totally gone now—
and was replaced by fury. Without
warning, he threw a hard right hook
to Barnes's jaw. Caught completely off
guard, the bigger kid rocked backward several steps.

The other eighth-graders edged
forward, ready to jump into the
fight, but Barnes waved them back.
Then he rushed at Will, shoving
him angrily to the ground. But Will
quickly scrambled back up and

socked the bigger kid in the stomach.

As Barnes stood doubled over, trying to breathe, the Bulls began to cheer.

The eighth-graders looked questioningly at their leader. "You okay, TB?" asked the one who had given Will the knee.

"Yeah, yeah," Barnes gasped, waving him off. Then he attacked Will again, punching him hard repeatedly on the left arm. But Will stood his ground and delivered an uppercut that caught 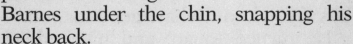 Barnes under the chin, snapping his neck back.

Barnes shook his head, checking for damage, then charged Will one more time, locking him in a clinch.

But Will managed to free his right arm and pounded away at the eighth-grader's ribs.

"Okay, okay," Barnes blurted, still gripping Will in a tight bear hug, "don't make me hurt you. You know I can re-arrange your face, but it wouldn't look so good if I did that to a fifth-grader."

"Want me to finish him off for you, TB?" his eager buddy offered.

"Nah, let him be," Barnes said, panting for breath. "The little dude put up a good fight. I didn't know he had it in him."

Will finally stopped punching, and Barnes released his grip. The two stood staring at each other, breathing hard. Gradually Will began to un-clench his fists.

"I'm gonna let you go this time, Hopwood," Barnes said finally. "But just be sure you stay in the front of the bus if you know what's good for you."

He turned to go, and his buddies followed. As they walked away, Barnes looked back over his shoulder, fixing Will with one more menacing glare.

As soon as the eighth-graders were out of earshot, Dave dropped his voice down low and mimicked, "I'm gonna let you go this time. . . ."

All the Bulls started to laugh—partly at Barnes, partly in relief. Things had been pretty tense for a while.

Then Jo crowed, "Just be sure you stay in the front of the bus if you know what's good for you!"

The laughter built. Soon Dave, Chunky, and Mark were actually rolling around on the ground in hysterics.

Will was laughing so hard he was almost crying. He hadn't laughed—*really* laughed—for a long time. He knew, in spite of that last menacing glare, that his troubles with Barnes were over.

Brian grew serious for a moment. "Will, man," he asked, "are you okay? We'll get you a new jersey for that torn one. Barnes roughed you up pretty good."

"I'm fine," Will assured Brian. "I

haven't felt better in weeks. It's just a couple of bruises."

"And he gave as good as he got!" Chunky shouted. "Where'd you pick up those deadly moves, Will? I'll bet it's been a long time since somebody slam-dunked Travis Barnes like that!"

"It's just the animal in me," Will joked. "Every once in a while I let it out."

As the laughter died down Will looked over at Brian. "Hey, Bri," he asked, "what were you thinking, having the Bulls follow me like that? Were you trying to start a gang war or something?"

"Nah," Brian said, sounding a little uncomfortable. "Listen, Will, you had to live with this thing by yourself long enough. You said you wanted to settle it on your own, and you did. But you remember what I told you during halftime?"

"Of course I do," Will answered. "You said that whatever I decided to do, the Bulls would be behind me." He looked around at all his team- mates. "And you were."

"Hey," said Brian, throwing his arm around Will's shoulder, "isn't that what friends are for?"

Don't miss Sup er Hoops #8,
Ball Hog, coming soon!

As Jo dribbled around the perimeter of their family's driveway, her brother Otto asked, "Did you know that of all of the Bulls' starters, you have the lowest scoring average? *Dead last.*"

She continued to dribble. "You know, scoring isn't everything, lamebrain," she said, trying to sound as though she didn't care if she *was* last. "I get just as much of a kick out of dishing the ball, and shutting my man down on D, as I do out of scoring."

Jo knew she didn't sound totally convincing. And the way Otto just kept smirking at her, as if he didn't believe a word she said, made her furious.

"Besides," she went on, "if I wanted to, I could outscore you any time." Having said that, Jo dribbled in just inside the foul line, stopped, and popped. *Good.*

"Ten–nine," she said, as if that settled the question.

Otto paid little attention to his sister's basket. "Oh, yeah?" he replied, absently checking the ball with Jo. "Why don't we see about that in two weeks, when the Bulls play the Slashers? We can play a little mano a mano—or is it mano a *girl-o?*"

He emphasized his challenge by draining a long jumper over Jo's outstretched arm.

Man, is he obnoxious! Jo found herself thinking for about the thousandth time. *It really would be great to outscore him in the Bulls-Slashers game, just to shut his mouth!*

About the Author

Hank Herman is a writer and newspaper columnist who lives in Connecticut with his wife, Carol, and their three sons, Matt, Greg, and Robby.

His column, "The Home Team," appears in the *Westport News*. It's about kids, sports, and life in the suburbs.

Although Mr. Herman was formerly the editor in chief of *Health* magazine, he now writes mostly about sports. At one time, he was a tennis teacher, and he has also run the New York City Marathon. He coaches kids' basketball every winter and Little League baseball every spring.

He runs, bicycles, skis, kayaks, and plays tennis and basketball on a regular basis. Mr. Herman admits that he probably spends about as much time playing, coaching, and following sports as he does writing.

Of all sports, basketball is his favorite.